MARTIN WADDE

The House Unde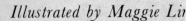
Stairs

Illustrated by Maggie Li

It's Grandad who shows Peter how to
play the House under the Stairs game.
Peter's mother is letting him use the
cupboard under the stairs as his own
special house. To play you stand outside
the cupboard door, spin round three
times, and say:

> 'Who is there
> Under the stair?'

Peter finds some very strange creatures,
and people too, making the house their
lair – a different one every day of the
week!

For Dominic Le Garsmeur
and Duncan Welford
who lent me their Pirate
and for Gina
who believed in him.

MARTIN WADDELL

The House
Under The Stairs

A Magnet Book

First published 1983 by Methuen Children's Books Ltd
Magnet paperback edition published 1984
by Methuen Children's Books Ltd,
11 New Fetter Lane, London EC4P 4EE
Text copyright © 1983 Martin Waddell
Illustrations copyright © 1983 Maggie Ling
Printed in Great Britain
by Cox & Wyman Ltd, Reading

ISBN 0 416 46170 0

Contents

1   The Monday Dragon

There were lots of people in Peter's house on the day when Mum came home from hospital with his new baby sister. There was Mum, Dad, baby Paula, Gran Potts and Grandad, Mrs. Adams-in-from-next-door, Peter, and Peter's cat, Felixstowe.

Peter got out his drum, and banged it in the hall.

'Peter! Stop that banging!' said Gran Potts. 'You'll wake the baby.'

Peter stopped banging his drum, and got out his train set instead.

'No, Peter!' said Gran Potts. 'We can't have you puff-puffing all over the sitting-room floor. Somebody might trip over you, and get hurt.'

Peter couldn't play upstairs, because Grandad was up there, having forty winks. So he got out one of his books and went to see if Dad would read to him, but Dad was too busy doing the dishes.

'What's the matter with my Peter?' Mum said, when Peter looked round the door of the bedroom, where she was taking a rest.

'I've got nowhere to play,' said Peter. 'Can I play in here?'

'Baby Paula is asleep, Peter,' said Mum, and she showed him the baby.

Peter had seen baby Paula before, and he didn't think much of her. She was small, and rather cross looking. Everybody kept saying *'Oh, what a lovely little baby sister you've got, Peter! Aren't you lucky?'* but Peter didn't think he was lucky at all. Peter thought baby Paula was a nuisance.

'Can I go outside?' Peter asked, but Mum said it was raining, and he would have to play inside.

'Where can I play?' Peter asked.

Mum thought about it, and then she had a good idea.

'We'll make you a special house, Peter,' she said.

8

'Where?' asked Peter.

'I'll give you a clue,' said Mum, getting out of bed and putting on her dressing-gown. 'It's a secret, hidden place. It has a little door, and you can make a house inside.'

'My cupboard?' guessed Peter, but he knew he couldn't make a house in his cupboard, because of Grandad and his forty winks.

'I'll show you,' said Mum. She took Peter

into the hall, and showed him the cupboard under the stairs.

'In there?' said Peter, peering through the little door.

'Yes,' said Mum. She got Dad to bring Peter's chair and his desk and his tea set, and put them in the tiny room under the stairs. Then Mrs. Adams-in-from-next-door put a notice on the door, pinned up with drawing pins. It said:

PETER'S HOUSE

in big red letters.

'There!' said Mum. 'You can play in there, Peter!' and she went back to bed.

'But not your drum!' said Gran Potts, who had come to look at Peter's new house.

Peter didn't play his drum. He put his Kangaroo and his Fat Ted and his Battleship in his new house, and he made himself an imaginary pot of tea, with a cup each for Kangaroo and Fat Ted and Battleship, although Mrs. Adams told him battleships didn't drink tea.

Then he got bored.

'What can I do now?' he asked Dad.

Dad gave him some crayons and a clean

sheet of Mum's typing paper, and told him to draw some pictures.

Peter drew a picture of Peter paddling for Mum, and a picture of Next Door for Mrs. Adams (with Mr. Adams standing on top of the roof) and then he got fed up drawing pictures.

'I'm fed up drawing pictures,' he said to Grandad, who had finished his forty winks and come downstairs to look at Peter's house. 'What can I do now?'

'I'll show you,' said Grandad. He brought Peter out of his house, and closed the little door under the stairs.

'We're going to do some magic, Peter,' he said.

'What sort of magic?' Peter asked.

'House-under-the-stairs magic, Peter,' said Grandad. 'This is what you do. First, you close your eyes. Then you spin round three times. Then you knock on the door of your house and say:

"WHO IS THERE UNDER THE STAIR?"

Then you open the door!'

'What happens then?' said Peter.

11

'You'll find somebody magic to play with in your house,' said Grandad.

'Will I?' asked Peter, who didn't really believe him.

'I always did,' said Grandad. 'Of course, it may not work for you. It only works for Special People.'

Peter wasn't sure whether he was a Special Person or not but he closed his eyes, spun round three times, said:

**'WHO IS THERE
UNDER THE STAIR?'**

in a very loud voice, and opened the door.

And ...

there ...

was a ...

DRAGON!

It was a blue and gold dragon, with smoke coming out of its ears and flames coming out of its mouth.

'Gosh!' said Peter, who had never seen a dragon before.

'Who is it?' asked Grandad.

'Can't you see?' said Peter.

'Only the owner of the House under the

stairs can see,' said Grandad. 'I thought you knew that.'

'It's a dragon,' said Peter.

'Ah,' said Grandad. 'The Monday Dragon! I remember now. It's always a dragon on Mondays.'

'Can I play with it?' asked Peter.

'Better ask it and see,' said Grandad.

'Can I play with you, Dragon?' Peter asked, and the Dragon said he could.

Peter made a cup of tea for the Dragon.

The Dragon drank it all up. There was a fizzing sound, the flames went out, and a lot of steam came out of the Dragon's ears.

'Pardon me!' said the Dragon politely.

Then the Dragon took Peter flying in the hall. It had short, scaly wings, and they flapped very fast.

ZOOOOOOOOM! went Peter up the hall, sitting on the Dragon's back. WOOO-OOOOOSH! they went up the stairs and PHAOOOOOH! down the stairs again.

'Peter!' said Gran Potts. 'What's all that noise about?'

'I'm flying on my Monday Dragon,' Peter said.

Gran Potts didn't believe him.

'No more noise, or you'll wake the baby!' she said, in a cross voice.

Peter told the Dragon, and the Dragon fizzed a bit and told Peter that it thought babies were silly.

'My Dragon thinks the baby is silly,' Peter told Mum.

'I didn't know that you had a dragon, Peter,' said Mum.

Peter told her about:

'WHO IS THERE UNDER THE STAIR?'

'Gran Potts says I can't fly on my Dragon because of the baby and my Dragon says babies are silly,' said Peter.

'Oh dear!' said Mum. 'What a pity.'

'Why is it a pity?'

'Well, you see, Peter,' said Mum, sitting up in bed, 'I was very pleased to hear you had a Dragon, because I thought it might be able to help me with a problem.'

'What sort of a problem?' asked Peter.

'Well,' said Mum, 'when baby Paula was in hospital, she was very warm all the time, because they had central heating. But now she's back in our house, and we haven't got central heating, have we? I thought your Dragon might help me to keep Paula cosy and warm.'

Peter wasn't certain if his Dragon wanted to have anything to do with babies.

'I don't think the Dragon would do it,' Peter said.

'I bet it would if *you* asked it,' said Mum, 'because it's your Dragon, isn't it? Nobody else's.'

Peter thought about it.

'I think my Dragon used to belong to Grandad,' he said.

'But now it belongs to you,' said Mum.

Peter said that he would ask his Dragon about keeping Paula warm, and he did.

'What does your Dragon say?' asked Mum.

'My Dragon says it'll help keep Paula warm after I've gone to bed, but it wants to play with me first,' said Peter.

'That's very kind of it,' said Mum. 'Thank you Peter, for lending baby Paula your Dragon.'

'You'll have to give it drinks,' said Peter. 'Drinks make it fizz. If it doesn't get drinks it'll start breathing fire, and baby Paula might be burnt up.'

16

'I'll have some special drinks for it, Peter,' promised Mum.

Mum was pleased, and Peter was pleased, and Grandad was especially pleased and even Gran Potts said she was pleased, although she didn't really believe in dragons. The Monday Dragon was *very* pleased, because it had pleased everybody, and was going to get special drinks to make it fizz instead of breathing fire.

'Dragonade is best,' said Gran Potts and she showed Peter how to make some, with fiery red raspberry juice and a lemon boat and ice cubes. Peter drank some and they left the rest in a jug by the bed, for Mum to give to the Dragon.

'Grandad,' said Peter, when Grandad came up to see him in bed. 'Grandad, will my Dragon still be there in the morning?'

'No, Peter,' said Grandad. 'It's the Monday Dragon, you see. It only comes on Mondays. There'll be someone quite different in the House under the stairs tomorrow.'

'Who?' said Peter.

'What day is tomorrow?' asked Grandad.

'Tuesday,' said Peter. 'Who comes on a Tuesday?'

17

'Ah,' said Grandad. 'That would be the Tuesday Witch.'

'Witch?' said Peter, who wasn't sure that he liked witches. 'What sort of a witch, Grandad?'

'Wait and see!' said Grandad.

2 The Tuesday Witch

Peter woke up on Tuesday morning, worrying about witches.

'I don't *think* I like witches,' he told Gran Potts, when she was helping him to get dressed.

'There are no such things, Peter!' said Gran Potts, firmly, and then she got Peter to show her how he could tie his shoe laces.

'Gran says that there are no such things as witches, Grandad,' Peter said, when he was talking to Grandad in the garden after breakfast.

'Does she?' said Grandad. 'Your Gran doesn't know everything Peter.'

'She knows a lot, though, doesn't she?" said Peter.

'Not about witches and dragons,' said Grandad.

Peter knew that Grandad was right. Gran didn't believe in dragons, and there had been a Monday Dragon. It was a helpful Dragon, and it played with Peter. But witches . . .

'Have you looked under the stairs this morning, Peter?' Grandad asked.

'I don't think I will, just yet,' said Peter, and he went off to play with Felixstowe. Usually Felixstowe was good at climbing the apple tree and catching mice, but today she didn't want to play.

'Felixstowe's getting very fat, Mum,' Peter said. 'She won't play with me. She just wants to sit.'

'I think Felixstowe is planning a surprise for us, one of these days, Peter,' said Mum.

'I want her to play *now*,' said Peter.

When he went back to the garden, Felixstowe had gone.

Next Peter went out in the car with Dad to fetch Paula's pram from the repair shop. It was Peter's old pram, with new springs.

'It looks fine!' Mum said, when they brought it back.

'It's my pram,' said Peter.

'But you don't mind baby Paula having it, do you?' said Mum. 'You're much too big for it now.'

'Paula can borrow it,' said Peter.

He went to look for Felixstowe again, but he couldn't find her. Then Gran Potts said he could help her to peel the potatoes.

Peter didn't feel like peeling potatoes.

'I'm going to play with Grandad,' he said, but Grandad was having forty winks.

Peter came down the stairs, and looked at the door of the House under the stairs. He opened it, and looked inside. Kangaroo and Fat Ted and Battleship were in there, but there was no sign of the Monday Dragon, or the Tuesday Witch.

She might be a nice witch, a good witch, but Peter wasn't sure.

Still . . .

He took a deep breath, and closed the door of the house under the stairs. Then he spun round three times, said:

'WHO IS THERE
UNDER THE STAIR?'

and opened the door.

It was dark inside the House under the

stairs, and at first Peter couldn't see anything.
Then . . .

. . . Peter saw something, glowing at him out of the darkness, down in the corner of the House under the stairs.

There were two *somethings*, like eyes, looking at him.

'Ooooh!' gasped Peter, and he shut the door quickly, in case the Tuesday Witch would get him.

'Mum!' said Peter. 'Mum. Come quick! There's a Bad Wicked Witch with glowing eyes under the stairs, Mum, in my house.'

'Is there?' said Mum. She was sitting with her feet up in the sitting-room, resting.

'Come and see, Mum,' said Peter.

Mum came out into the hall.

'I don't see any witch,' she said.

'Open the door, Mum,' said Peter, and he stood behind Mum's legs as she opened the door of the House under the stairs.

'There!' said Peter, pointing inside, but not daring to look.

'Felixstowe!' said Mum.

'What?' said Peter.

'That wasn't a Wicked Witch under the stairs, Peter,' said Mum. 'It was Felixstowe!

Cats' eyes glow in the dark, you know. Felix-stowe was having forty winks, like Grandad, with Kangaroo and Fat Ted and Battleship.'

'Isn't there any Bad Wicked Witch?' asked Peter, who didn't know whether to be relieved or disappointed.

'None at all,' said Mum.

Peter thought about it.

'I'd better ask Grandad,' he said.

'Wait till Grandad wakes up!' said Mum, and she went back to the sitting-room. Peter went with her and watched Playschool, and then Grandad came downstairs.

'Peter was worried about a Bad Wicked Witch under the stairs, Grandad,' said Mum. 'He says you told him there would be one.'

'No I didn't,' said Grandad.

'Yes you did,' said Peter. 'The Tuesday Witch!' Mum told Grandad all about Felix-stowe, and the glowing eyes.

'Peter thought it was a Wicked Witch,' said Mum.

'The Tuesday Witch isn't wicked!' said Grandad. 'She's nice, as witches go.'

'I *thought* she would be,' said Mum.

'*How* do witches go, Grandad?' asked Peter, anxiously.

'Well,' said Grandad. 'She *is* a witch and you have to be very careful with witches. You mustn't offend her. But normally she's the sweetie-giving kind of witch.'

'Oh,' said Peter, who had never heard of a sweetie-giving witch before.

'Let's go and see if she's there,' said Grandad.

They went to the House under the stairs, and Peter told Grandad about spinning round and saying:

'WHO IS THERE
UNDER THE STAIR?'

'There was nobody there but Felixstowe, and Kangaroo, and Fat Ted and Battleship,' said Peter.

'Not up and about yet, I expect,' said Grandad. 'Lazy lot, these witches. Have another go.'

So Peter had another go.

He closed his eyes, spun round three times and said:

'WHO IS THERE
UNDER THE STAIR?'

Nobody!

'Oh dear,' said Grandad. 'What's hap-pened?'

He looked inside Peter's House under the stairs.

'You won't be able to see her, Grandad,' said Peter. 'Only the owner of the House under the stairs can see.'

'I know,' said Grandad. 'But look what I've found!'

It was a sweetie.

Grandad found it sitting beside Kangaroo, where the Tuesday Witch had left it.

It was a red, sugary sweet, the sort Gran Potts said would rot Peter's teeth.

'Witches have rotten teeth anyway,' said Grandad. 'Better eat it, Peter. You don't want to offend her.'

Peter ate it. It was nice.

He looked for some more, and found one, in Battleship's tea-cup.

'The Tuesday Witch must like you, Peter,' said Grandad. 'I expect she was sorry she missed you the first time, and left the sweeties instead.'

'Where is she?' asked Peter.

'She'll be about the place somewhere,' said Grandad.

Peter went to look.

'Have you seen the Tuesday Witch?' he asked Mrs. Adams next door, but she hadn't. Neither had Gran Potts, but Dad said the Tuesday Witch might be playing with Felixstowe, because witches like cats, and that is where she was.

The Tuesday Witch had a big black hat, and a broomstick, and very, very bad teeth from eating too many sweets.

'You should have false teeth that grow in a glass, like Gran Potts,' said Peter, sitting down beside her under the apple tree.

'I like my own rotten ones best,' said the Tuesday Witch.

They played witch games in the garden for ages, and then Dad said it was time for lunch.

There were six places laid at the table.

One for Mum. One for Dad. One for Gran Potts. One for Grandad. One for Peter. And one next to Peter's.

'I laid a place for your Witch, Peter,' said Grandad.

Peter went out into the garden and brought the Tuesday Witch in and she said that he was to thank Grandad very much.

'My Witch says thank you very much, Grandad,' said Peter.

'Not at all,' said Grandad. 'It's my pleasure, Peter.'

Dinner was salad, with sardines.

'I don't think witches *like* sardines,' said Peter. He wasn't very fond of sardines himself.

'Witches *love* sardines,' said Gran Potts. And she put three sardines on the Tuesday Witch's plate, but no lettuce or tomato or cheese or beetroot or potato.

'Tell her, no spells at table,' said Grandad. 'Spells turn the cream sour, and you'll want some cream on your strawberries.'

'Are there strawberries?' asked Peter.

'After you've finished your sardine salad!' said Gran Potts, firmly.

Peter ate his lettuce and his tomato and some of his potato and his beetroot and was halfway through his cheese when Gran Potts had to rush out and answer the doorbell. When she came back in again, Peter's plate was empty.

'Strawberries, please!' said Peter.

'Did you finish your sardines?' asked Gran Potts, suspiciously.

'Well, not exactly,' said Peter.

'Where are they?'

'We gave them to the Tuesday Witch,' said Grandad.

Gran Potts looked at the Witch's plate. There were six sardines on it.

'You said witches liked sardines,' Grandad explained. 'And the Tuesday Witch only had three, so Peter thought he would give her his three as well, because she didn't have lettuce or tomato or cheese or beetroot or potato.'

Gran Potts didn't say anything, but she gave Peter strawberries and cream.

'Walk time!' said Gran Potts, when they had all finished eating.

Peter didn't want to go walking with Gran Potts, who walked very fast, but Mum said he should go, so he went, and the Tuesday Witch went with him.

They went to the library. Gran Potts changed her books, and Peter changed his and the Tuesday Witch sat on the big ladybird cushion on the floor and went to sleep.

After the library, they had to go to the Post Office, and after the Post Office they went to the Supermarket where Gran Potts told the lady at the check-out all about Peter's lovely new baby sister Paula, and what a lucky boy Peter was.

'Gran!' said Peter.

'Don't interrupt, Peter,' said Gran Potts, and she went on talking.

'Gran! We forgot the Witch.'

'What?' said Gran Potts, in a cross voice.

'We left her in the library, Gran,' said Peter.

'Who?' said the check-out lady.

'One of Peter's little friends,' said Gran, sounding embarrassed.

'We'll have to go and get her, *quickly*,' said Peter.

But Gran Potts wouldn't go back to the library. She said the Tuesday Witch could look after herself.

'She doesn't know the way!' said Peter.

'Of course she does,' said Gran Potts.

They went home.

'Where is my Witch?' Peter asked, after he'd looked in the House under the stairs.

'I expect she'll show up quite soon,' said Gran Potts. 'Like a bad penny.'

But the Tuesday Witch didn't.

'I've lost the Tuesday Witch!' Peter told Grandad.

'Oh dear, she won't be pleased,' said Grandad, rubbing his chin.

'Gran made me leave her in the library!' said Peter.

'I did no such thing!' said Gran.

'Yes, you did!' said Peter. 'You said we were in too much of a hurry to go back.'

'Let's go and look for her, Peter,' said Grandad.

They walked down to the garden gate, and looked down the street.

'Any sign?' said Grandad, hopefully.

There was a sudden flurry of wind, and the hedge rippled.

'There she is!' said Peter, and he went to greet the Tuesday Witch, who was looking a bit puffed after the long walk home.

The Tuesday Witch was pleased to be back. She went into the sitting-room and sat down, to rest her feet. They were big feet, in black shiny shoes with buckle, which had become rather dusty with walking.

'All right now, Peter?' said Dad, who had been told all about it by Gran Potts.

'Yes,' said Peter.

Then Dad sat down.

'Don't sit there, Dad,' said Peter, quickly.

'Why?'

'You're sitting on my Tuesday Witch!' said Peter.

'I do beg your pardon, Madam,' said Dad, and he went to sit down on the other arm-chair.

After tea, Gran Potts read Peter a story, Dad gave him his bath and then Mum put him to bed.

'Shush, Mum,' said Peter, as they opened the bedroom door. 'Don't wake the Witch!'

32

'Do you think she's asleep?' asked Mum.
They tip-toed into the room.
The Tuesday Witch wasn't there.
'Oh, Mum!' said Peter, in a disappointed voice.
'Never mind, Peter,' said Mum.
'I expect she was cross because Gran Potts gave her sardines she doesn't like and lost her at the library and then Dad sat on her,' Peter said.
'What a pity,' said Mum, in a tired voice.
'I'd better go down and see if I can find her,' said Peter. 'Grandad says you mustn't offend witches.'
'You stay where you are,' said Mum. 'I'll speak to Grandad about it.'
She came back in about five minutes.
'Did you speak to Grandad?' Peter asked.
'No,' said Mum. 'I went one better. I spoke to the Tuesday Witch.'
'You can't see her!' said Peter.
'She let me see her,' said Mum. 'Witches can do that if they want to. She's a very polite witch, I must say. Do you know what she said?'
'What did she say?' asked Peter.
'She said, "Thank you very much for a good

time, and the sardines, and see you next Tuesday,"' said Mum.

'But she doesn't like sardines.'

'Yes she does,' said Mum. 'Your Gran was right about that. The Tuesday Witch *loves* sardines, but she likes them mashed up, so that there aren't any scrunchy bits. She doesn't like eating the scrunchy bits because of her bad teeth, you see.'

'Oh,' said Peter.

'So I mashed them up for her, and left them in the House under the stairs,' said Mum.

'Can I go and look?' asked Peter.

He went downstairs to the hall, and looked.

There was the Tuesday Witch's plate, and a napkin, but not a trace of sardine ... the Tuesday Witch had swallowed every one.

And there was a bad-for-your-teeth sweetie, left specially for Peter.

3 The Wednesday Wozzle

It was Wednesday morning and Mum, Dad and Grandad had taken baby Paula out in the car to meet Aunt Phyllis. Peter was left at home to look after Gran Potts and Felixstowe.

Gran Potts decided to have one of her busy mornings, which she couldn't have when Mum was around because Mum kept saying, *'Do sit down Gran, you're making me nervous.'*

'This house is in a shocking state!' Gran Potts said. She made Peter clear all his boats out of the bath and put them back in the plastic basin, and then she made him carry his train set and his blocks upstairs, and then she chased Felixstowe out of the polish box, where the cat had made a little bed. Then Gran Potts got out some dusters and the polish and she went round humming and singing and banging and lifting and making such a disturbance that Peter couldn't get peace to read.

Peter couldn't really read, but he knew all the pictures in his picture book, and the stories that went with them, and he enjoyed reading to Kangaroo.

'No toys on the sofa, dear!' Gran Potts said. 'I'm just getting the place spick and span for your mother.'

Peter took Kangaroo back up to his own room, and left him talking to Felixstowe, who had come up to hide under the bed.

Peter went downstairs again and got out his bubble pipe and bubble mixture.

Peter was good at blowing bubbles. He blew six small blue ones, and then three all clustered together, and then he blew a big, big, BIG one that got bigger and bigger. The bubble took off and floated out of the kitchen, with Peter running after it. It floated down the hall, just as Gran Potts came bustling out of the sitting-room door.

POP!

The bubble burst, right in front of Gran Potts' face. Gran Potts jumped, and her glasses jumped too, and came down crooked on her nose.

'You look funny, Gran!' Peter said.

Gran Potts didn't think it was funny at all.

'Outside, Peter, if you're going to play messy games like that!' she said, firmly.

'I don't want to go outside,' said Peter.

'Then sit down quietly in the front room and watch television,' said Gran Potts.

'Don't want to,' said Peter.

'Go and play in your House under the stairs,' said Gran Potts.

Peter thought about it.

He had been deliberately staying away from the House under the stairs because it was Wednesday, and he didn't know who might be in there on a Wednesday. The Monday Dragon had been nice, and the Tuesday Witch had turned out all right in the end, but he had forgotten to ask Grandad about Wednesday.

He could, of course, have gone into the House under the stairs without closing his eyes and spinning round three times and saying:

**'WHO IS THERE
UNDER THE STAIR?'**

37

Somehow that didn't seem a very brave thing to do.

It could be ... what? A tiger that ate little boys. A Wicked Wizard. A Monster.

Peter didn't know, but he decided that he ought to find out.

He closed his eyes, spun round three times, and said:

'WHO IS THERE UNDER THE STAIR?'

Peter opened the door of the House under the stairs.

'Oh!' said Peter. 'Hullo!'

'Hullo,' said someone in a deep voice. 'Pleased to meet you, Peter.'

'Who are you?' Peter asked.

'I'm a Wozzle,' the voice replied. 'The Wednesday Wozzle.'

The Wednesday Wozzle was fat and furry, like a polar bear, and it had a small cuddly Wozzle baby with it.

'Is that your baby?' Peter asked.

'Shssh!' said the Wednesday Wozzle. 'You'll waken it.'

Peter was very, very quiet, and he went into his House under the stairs with the Wozzle and the Baby Wozzle and made the Wozzle a cup of tea, using his tea set.

Gran Potts started hoovering in the hall.

The door of the House under the stairs opened, and Peter's head popped out. 'Gran?' he said. 'GRAN!'

'What is it, Peter?' said Gran.

'Please, could you stop hoovering, Gran. You'll wake the baby,' Peter said.

'Don't be silly, Peter,' said Gran Potts. 'The baby is out in the car with your mother.'

'Not *that* baby!' said Peter, 'the Wednesday Wozzle's baby.'

'Wozzle?' said Gran Potts. What's a wozzle? 'I don't think that I believe in Wozzles, but I've only a tiny bit left to do in the hall, so perhaps you would explain to your Wozzle.'

She went on hoovering, until she was satisfied that the hall was clean and then she went into the kitchen to have a cup of tea.

'You wakened the baby!' Peter said, putting his head round the door. 'Now it won't go to sleep!'

'Give it a feed,' Gran Potts said, and she made up one of baby Paula's bottles for the Wozzle baby.

'Thank you very much, Gran,' Peter said. He took the bottle back to the House under the stairs, where he gave it to the Wozzle, who fed it to the baby.

Mum, Dad, Grandad and baby Paula came back for lunch, and after lunch Grandad had his nap upstairs and when he came downstairs he found Kangaroo and Fat Ted and Battleship sitting on cushions in the hall, while Peter rushed up and down kicking his ball.

'What are you doing, Peter?' Grandad said. 'Better not let your Gran catch you at it, after she's spent all morning tidying.'

'This is a football match, Grandad,' Peter explained.

'They don't look as if they're playing football,' Grandad said, looking at Kangaroo and Fat Ted and Battleship.

'They're not,' said Peter. 'They're only watching. The football match is between me and the Wozzle's baby and the Wozzle. The Wozzle's baby is on my side, because we are both small, and we are beating the Wozzle.'

'How many by?' Grandad asked.

'Two goals to one,' said Peter. 'I got one goal, and the Wozzle's baby got the other.'

'Most babies don't play football,' Grandad said.

'The Wozzle's baby is a brilliant footballer!' said Peter. 'Much better than Paula.'

'Paula is too small to play football yet,' said Grandad.

'The Wozzle's baby is small too,' said Peter, and he went on with his football match.

Peter and Wozzle's baby beat the Wozzle by six goals to three, and then Peter and the Wozzle's baby went out into the garden

and climbed the tree, and then the Wozzle said it was time for the baby to have another feed.

'Can I have another feed for the baby please, Mum?' Peter asked, taking the empty bottle into the sitting-room.

'Can I see the baby?' Mum said, after she had filled the bottle for Peter.

'Sorry,' said Peter. 'I'm the only one who can see it.'

'Oh. I thought if you asked the Wozzle specially, he might let me see it,' said Mum. 'I like babies.'

'The Wozzle's baby is much better than Paula, Mum,' said Peter. 'The Wozzle's baby plays football, and climbs trees. Paula can't do that, can she?'

'She will be able to when she grows up,' said Mum.

'Really?' said Peter.

'Yes. And you can teach her to play football and climb trees, can't you?'

'Yes,' said Peter. 'Yes, I can.'

'Paula will be very proud of her big brother,' said Mum.

'I can't teach her yet though, can I?' said Peter. 'Paula is too small.'

'No,' said Mum. 'But you can help me to look after her, and keep her safe, can't you?'

'I will!' said Peter, and he went off to tell the Wozzle about it, and the Wozzle thought it was a good idea.

4 The Thursday Robber

Gran Potts woke up on Thursday morning, and couldn't find her teeth.

They were shiny, white, plastic teeth fixed to a pink inner plate which fitted inside her mouth. They were very real-looking. Each night, before she went to sleep, Gran Potts put them beside the bed in a glass filled with a special mixture that cleaned them, and each morning she popped them back into her mouth, first thing. But on Thursday morning, her teeth were missing.

'No teef!' she squeaked, jabbing Grandad in the ribs. She couldn't speak very well without her teeth, and everything she said ended with a sort of whistle.

'In your tooth glass,' Grandad muttered, still half asleep.

'No glaff!' Gran Potts said.

'No glass?' said Grandad, sitting up and looking. There was no tooth-glass in the usual place beside the bed.

'No teef! No glaff!' said Gran Potts, sounding very upset.

'You must have left them somewhere. Better look for them,' Grandad said.

'No teef!' said Gran Potts. 'I'm not going downstairs wiffout my teef!'

Gran Potts was a tidy person, who tried very hard to look neat all the time. She didn't want people to see her going around the house without her teeth, whistling when she spoke.

'Pleef look for my teef!' Gran Potts said.

Grandad loved Gran Potts very much, and he didn't want her to feel embarrassed, so he climbed out of bed, put on his dressing-gown and slippers, and went padding off through the house to look for her teeth.

Peter had been downstairs helping Mum to change baby Paula and having a special cuddle, and he met Grandad coming down the stairs.

'Good morning, Peter,' said Grandad. 'You haven't seen Gran's teeth, have you?'

46

'Yes I have,' said Peter.

'Where?' asked Grandad, hopefully.

'In her mouth where they always are,' said Peter. 'I saw them yesterday.'

'That's not what I meant,' said Grandad, and he told Peter about the missing teeth. 'When she speaks, she whistles, like this!' Grandad said, and he said 'Teef!' and whistled.

'Does she?' said Peter, and he went off to hear Gran Potts whistle, but Gran Potts pulled the bed clothes over her head, and wouldn't say a word, or whistle even a little bit.

Grandad couldn't find Gran Potts' teeth, though he looked everywhere he could think of, in the kitchen, in the bathroom, in the sitting-room and under the bed.

'Can't you remember where you put them?' he asked impatiently.

'My good teef!' Gran Potts grumbled, but she couldn't remember.

Gran Potts wouldn't come down to breakfast, because she said she couldn't eat without her teeth.

'Will Gran starve and die?' Peter asked anxiously. Grandad wasn't the only one who loved Gran Potts. Peter loved her too, and he didn't want her to starve and die, even if she was cross with him sometimes.

'I expect we'll find her teeth first,' Dad said, and Mum said nobody would let Gran starve and die, she was much too nice a Gran for that.

'We'll have a Great Teeth Hunt!' said Grandad, and after breakfast Grandad, Peter, Mum and Dad went teeth hunting. They found four marbles and Peter's yellow underpants under his bed, and Felixstowe making herself a little house in Mum's briefcase, but they didn't find Gran's teeth.

Then Mum had to go and fix Paula's bottle, and Dad had to go out and buy some new socks and Peter and Grandad were left to go hunting alone.

'I'm tired of Teeth Hunting!' Peter said, when they had finished searching round the bathroom a second time.

'So am I,' said Grandad. 'But you see, Peter, we'll have to keep looking because it is *sort of* our fault.'

'Why?' asked Peter.

'Well,' said Grandad. 'I think I know what has happened to them.'

'What has?' asked Peter.

48

'The Thursday Robber!' said Grandad.

'Thursday Robber!' gasped Peter.

'This is Thursday, isn't it?' Grandad asked, and Peter said it was. 'Well then,' said Grandad. 'That's what's happened, I'm afraid. The Thursday Robber has got hold of them, and hidden them away. And there wouldn't have been any Thursday Robber if it hadn't been for us, and the House under the stairs' magic, would there, Peter?'

'I didn't spin round, or anything,' Peter said.

'The Thursday Robber doesn't always wait for that, I'm afraid,' said Grandad. 'He's not a very nice person, the Thursday Robber. He takes things, and hides them away where nobody can find them. I bet that's what he's done with Gran's teeth.'

'Let's go and have a look at him,' Peter said, because he had never seen a robber.

'All right,' said Grandad. 'Just a quick one. Then we'll have to start searching again, or poor Gran will never be able to get up out of bed.'

They went into the hall and Peter closed his eyes, spun round three times, and said:

'WHO IS THERE
UNDER THE STAIR?'

He knew quite well who was there, before he opened the door, but he didn't know what the Thursday Robber would look like.

The Thursday Robber looked very nasty. He was big, and strong, and he had a red jersey, a cap pulled down over his eyes, and a bag under his arm.

Peter told Grandad about the bag and Grandad said they should look inside it so Peter chased the robber out of the House under the stairs, caught him, and looked in the bag.

'Are they there?' Grandad asked.

The teeth weren't there.

'Ask him where he's put them,' Grandad said.

'Where have you put Gran Potts' teeth?' Peter asked.

'I'm not telling!' the Thursday Robber said, with a grin. When he grinned, Peter saw his teeth. They were bright, shiny ones.

'I think the Thursday Robber is wearing Gran's teeth!' he told Grandad but Grandad said no, he couldn't be, because the dentist

had made Gran's teeth specially for her, and they wouldn't fit anyone else.

'We'll just have to keep on looking, I'm afraid, Peter,' said Grandad.

They did.

And Peter FOUND the teeth!

They were sitting out at the front door, in their glass, beside the milk-bottles.

'Left out with the milk bottles!' Grandad said, and he gave Gran Potts her teeth.

Gran Potts went red in the face, slipped her teeth in and said, 'I do feel a fool!'

'You're not a fool, Gran,' Peter said. 'It was the Thursday Robber! He hid your teeth out with the milk bottles, and he would have got away with it, if I hadn't found them!'

'I think he's right you know,' Grandad said, sounding very serious. 'Well done, Peter!'

'Very well done, Peter,' said Gran Potts. Then she told Peter not to say anything about where the Thursday Robber had hidden her teeth, and she gave him 10p for being a good boy and finding them.

Peter was very pleased.

So was Dad, when Peter showed him the 10p, and told him about being a good finder.

But Dad wasn't pleased when the Thursday Robber took his pen.

'I must have left it upstairs,' Dad said, but it wasn't upstairs.

'The Thursday Robber took it, but I found it!' Peter announced, producing the pen.

'Well done, Peter,' said Dad, and he gave Peter 5p.

The Thursday Robber took Grandad's slippers. Peter found them and Grandad gave Peter a sweet.

The Thursday Robber took Mum's knitting needles. Peter found them. Mum gave Peter a special big kiss she had been saving for him and then she said: 'Tell the Thursday Robber he's not to take any more things, Peter, or there will be trouble.'

'You're not to take any more things, Robber,' Peter told the Thursday Robber, but the Thursday Robber wouldn't listen.

He took Paula's red rabbit. It was a squeaky red rabbit. Mrs. Adams had given it to Paula, and she had given Peter some sweets at the same time, but Peter had eaten his sweets.

'Where's Paula's rabbit?' Mum said, and everybody looked at Peter.

'I expect the Thursday Robber took it,' Peter said.

Grandad looked cross. 'You tell your Thursday Robber that the Friday Policeman is coming tomorrow!' he said.

'What's he like?' said Peter.

'Very big and fierce,' said Grandad. 'He doesn't like robbers at all.'

'He likes finders, doesn't he?' said Peter.

'Yes,' said Grandad.

Peter found Paula's red rabbit, and gave it back to Paula. Peter was cross with the Thursday Robber, and the Thursday Robber promised that he would never steal anything again.

'Mum,' said Peter, when it was time for bed. 'I didn't like the Thursday Robber, did you?'

'Not a bit,' said Mum.

'He wasn't a real robber, was he? He was only pretend.'

'For a *pretend* robber, he did a lot of *real* taking!' Mum said.

'He didn't take Gran Potts' teeth, Mum,' Peter said. 'Gran Potts left them out herself, when she was leaving out the milk bottles.'

'Did she?' said Mum.

'Yes, she did,' said Peter.

54

'Well, don't tell Gran Potts we know,' said Mum. 'She might feel silly.'

'I won't tell,' said Peter.

'And we won't say any more about who really took Dad's pen and Grandad's slippers and my knitting needles and Paula's squeaky red rabbit,' said Mum. 'It's all forgiven and forgotten.'

'Yes, Mum,' said Peter, and Mum gave him another big kiss.

Mum went downstairs and Peter cuddled up in his big bed, with Felixstowe for company. Mum hadn't seen Felixstowe, who had been hiding away behind the curtains. She hopped up on the end of Peter's bed and purred at him. She had quite a lot to tell Peter about the special surprise she was planning, but Peter went to sleep before she could make him understand.

5   The Friday Policeman

Friday turned out to be one of Gran Potts' busy days.

First, she set the washing machine washing.

Then, she washed all the dishes a second time, because Dad hadn't been washing them properly.

Then, she chased all the toys upstairs.

Then, she chased Felixstowe downstairs, from the secret bed the cat had made for herself in the airing cupboard.

Then, she dusted everything she could find to dust, including Grandad's bald head, which happened to be in the way.

'That was me!' Grandad said, sitting up from his snooze, which he had been quietly enjoying in the soft chair in the sitting room.

'I know!' said Gran Potts. 'You're in my way!'

Grandad went off upstairs.

Gran tidied up Dad's tools.

'You're driving everybody mad, Mum,' Dad said, (for, of course, Gran Potts was *his* Mum, before he grew up to be Dad, and she was still *Mum* as far as he was concerned, although everybody else called her Gran Potts).

'I've got to leave everything spick and span!' said Gran Potts, puffing past with an armful of clean nappies.

'Is Gran Potts going somewhere, Dad?' Peter asked.

'Gran and Grandad are going home on Sunday,' Dad said. 'I bet you'll miss your old Gran, won't you?'

Peter thought about it.

Gran Potts walked too fast and in between walking fast she stopped and talked to people for ages and ages. She was always fussing about something and she made him brush his teeth four times a day and wash behind his ears and take all his toys upstairs. He decided that he wouldn't miss *that* Gran Potts at all.

But there was *another* Gran Potts. She read

him stories, bought him comics, made him nice fizzy drinks in the kitchen and told him he was her real darling and baby Paula didn't make any difference, except that she had two darlings now, instead of one.

'Yes, I will miss Gran,' said Peter, and he gave Gran Potts a big hug, when she came downstairs again.

'You'll all get a little peace when I'm gone!' said Gran Potts, and then she chased Peter and Dad out of the kitchen so that she could get on with things.

Peter went looking for Grandad. Grandad couldn't have his forty winks upstairs because Gran Potts had taken all the things out of the cupboard and put them on the bed, so he had taken Dad's deckchair out to the garden and he was snoozing in it, with Felixstowe on his knee.

'Wake up, Grandad!' Peter said. 'I want to play.'

'I refuse to wake up,' said Grandad, without opening his eyes.

'What about the Friday Policeman?' asked Peter.

'I don't know. I'm asleep,' said Grandad, and he wouldn't say any more.

'Grandad's in the garden and he won't wake up!' Peter told Mum.

'What?' said Mum, anxiously. She was afraid that something might have happened to Grandad.

'He says he won't wake up,' said Peter.

'Oh,' said Mum, sounding relieved. 'That's all right then.'

'No it's not,' said Peter. 'I want to see the Friday Policeman.'

'You don't need Grandad for that, do you?'

Peter explained that the Friday Policeman was big and fierce.

'Maybe he's not,' said Mum. 'I bet he's a nice policeman, who plays games.'

'Do you think so?' said Peter.

'Go and find out,' said Mum.

So Peter went to the house, closed his eyes, spun round three times, and said:

'WHO IS THERE UNDER THE STAIR?'

and something went *Peeep! Peeeep! Peeeeeeeeeep!*

Peter opened the door of the House under the stairs, and the Friday Policeman came riding out on his bright red bicycle with a sign saying:

60

hanging from a string round the handlebars.

Peeep! Peeeeep! Peeeeeeep! went the Friday Policeman's whistle.

Grandad had been wrong about the Friday Policeman. He wasn't big and fierce, he was small and roly-poly, and he rode up and down the hall on his bicycle pedalling very fast with his little fat legs, and blowing his whistle.

'Hop on the bike, Peter!' he called, and Peter hopped up on the bike behind him and they went Peeeep! Peeep! up and down the hall, and Peeep! Peeeep! into the sitting room and round the sofa, and Peeep! Peeeep! out of the sitting-room again and Peeeep! Peeep! into the kitchen and . . .

CRASH!

Right into Gran Potts' mop bucket.

The mop bucket tumbled over, and dirty water went all over Gran Potts' clean floor.

In the middle of the water was Peter, and beside Peter was the Friday Policeman. The Friday Policeman's whistle had got water in it, and instead of going

Peeep! Peeep!

it went

Fuuuuuuuup! Fuuuuuuup!

'Peter!' said Gran Potts, and she picked up the dripping Peter and carried him off upstairs to change his clothes.

The Friday Policeman went away and hid, where Gran Potts couldn't find him. He didn't want to be blamed for flooding the kitchen.

'It was the Friday Policeman!' Peter tried to explain to Gran Potts, but Gran Potts wasn't pleased, and she said he was to be a much more careful boy in future, and not go running round the house knocking over buckets.

Peter told Gran Potts he was very very sorry Gran Potts told him it was all right and gave him a big hug. Then she said that she was busy, and made Peter promise not to get up to any more mischief.

It wasn't Peter who got up to mischief, it was the Friday Policeman.

Peter found him hiding upstairs, beneath Grandad's bed, and on the way downstairs the Friday Policeman blew his whistle loudly, and that wakened baby Paula.

Baby Paula started to cry.

'It wasn't me, Mum,' said Percy. 'It was the Friday Policeman.'

Then the Friday Policeman decided he was

going to lock up all the toys in his jail in the House under the stairs.

Kangaroo and Fat Ted and Battleship fitted in all right, but after they were in, the Friday Policeman decided he was going to lock up all the sitting-room cushions as well.

Peter helped the Friday Policeman to get all the cushions rounded up and then the cushions said they didn't want to be locked up. They jumped on the Friday Policeman and there was a big fight with the cushions in the hall and Peter and the Friday Policeman were winning when one of the cushions burst.

'Grandad,' said Peter. 'Have you wakened up yet?'

'No,' said Grandad. 'I'm still fast asleep.'

'One of the cushions burst, and there are feathers all over the hall, Grandad,' Peter said.

Grandad opened one eye.

'Who burst the cushion, Peter?' he asked.

'The Friday Policeman!' Peter said.

'Does Gran Potts know?' Grandad asked, and Peter told him that Gran Potts had gone out to the shops.

'Perhaps we can tidy it up before she gets

back!' said Grandad. 'Then nobody will get into trouble, will they?'

Grandad and Peter went inside the house and started cleaning up.

Then they heard Gran Potts' key turning in the front door.

'Oh dear,' said Grandad.

Gran Potts wasn't at all pleased when she saw the mess in the hall. She was very cross with Grandad and Peter and the Friday Policeman, and the Friday Policeman ran away.

Peter and Grandad went out to the garden. Gran Potts said they were to stay there, and not make any more trouble.

'Your Friday Policeman is a funny sort of policeman, Peter,' said Grandad, scratching his bald head. 'He's always getting into trouble.'

'He gets me into trouble,' said Peter.

'I know he does,' said Grandad. 'Policemen are supposed to help people and get them out of trouble, not kick over mop buckets and burst cushions and wake babies up. You should get your Friday Policeman to do something helpful for a change, and not upset your Gran.'

'I'll get him to do something nice and kind, that will please Gran,' said Peter.

'That's a very good idea,' said Grandad.

Peter went looking for the Friday Policeman, but he couldn't find him. The Friday Policeman wasn't in the House under the stairs with Kangaroo and Fat Ted and Battleship. He wasn't in the airing cupboard, he wasn't hiding in the sitting-room behind the sofa, and he wasn't behind the curtains.

'What are you doing in here, Peter?' said Gran Potts. 'Your Mum is resting, and I told you to stay outside, out of my way.'

Peter told her that he was looking for the Friday Policeman.

'Perhaps he's out in the garden,' said Gran Potts.

Peter went out into the garden and he saw the Friday Policeman's red bicycle sitting at the bottom of the apple tree. The Friday Policeman had climbed up the tree and he was hiding there, but when he saw Peter he went Peeep! Peeep! on his whistle.

'The Friday Policeman is up the apple tree, hiding from Gran because she was cross,' said Peter.

'Is he?' said Grandad. 'Go and play with

him then, Peter. I want to finish my forty winks.'

'When you've had all your winks you can come and play with me,' said Peter.

'That's right,' said Grandad, and closed his eyes again and settled down in the deckchair.

Peter climbed up the apple tree.

'I want you to do something nice and kind for Gran Potts,' he told the Friday Policeman. 'To make up for you being bad.'

The Friday Policeman said he was sorry about being bad and he would try to think of something that would please Gran Potts.

They sat in the tree and they thought, and then the Friday Policeman had an idea. The Friday Policeman's idea was to pick a bag full of apples for Gran Potts.

Peter thought that it was a great idea, because it would save Gran Potts going out to the shop to buy apples if she felt like eating some.

'What are you looking for, Peter?' Mum said. She was in the kitchen heating Paula's bottle.

'I want a bag, Mum,' Peter said.

'What do you want it for, Peter?' Mum said, giving him a big, brown bag.

'It's a secret, Mum,' said Peter. 'A special surprise for Gran Potts.'

Peter and the Friday Policeman climbed up the apple tree and picked as many apples as they could. Peter was a better picker than the Friday Policeman because the Friday Policeman kept stopping to blow his whistle, just to keep in practice.

Peter had another idea. He decided to paint a picture for Gran Potts, and he climbed down the tree with the bag of apples and went into the kitchen, where he got out his paints, and his paint brush, and some paper, and filled his red egg cup full of water from the tap.

'Painting, Peter?' asked Dad.

'I'm painting a special picture for Gran Potts,' said Peter, proudly.

'What is it a picture of?' asked Dad.

'It's a present from me and the Friday Policeman,' said Peter. 'I've drawn Grandad sleeping in Dad's chair, and the Friday Policeman climbing up the apple tree and me sitting on the Friday Policeman's red bicycle, and that's Gran Potts in the kitchen being cross.'

'I don't think Gran Potts would be pleased

if you painted her cross,' said Dad. 'Why don't you make her smiley, instead?'

'I will,' said Peter, and he sploshed some paint on Gran Potts and made her smiley. Then he bumped into the egg cup with his elbow, and the paint water went *swish*, all over the table.

'Oh dear,' said Peter.

'What a mess!' said Dad, watching the water drip off the table on to Gran Potts' nice clean floor.

Gran Potts picked that moment to come back into the kitchen.

'PETER! What have you done now!' said Gran Potts, sounding really cross.

'It was my fault,' said Dad.

'It was Dad's fault,' agreed Peter.

'It's Peter's paint water!' said Gran Potts. 'I've had enough of Peter's messes for one day, I really have!'

'Don't be cross,' said Dad. 'Peter was painting a picture of you being smiley and friendly. He didn't think you would be pleased if he painted you cross, so he was using his imagination and painting you happy!'

'A smiley me, not a cross one?' said Gran Potts.

'You're much nicer when you're not being cross,' said Peter.

'I'm only cross when I have to be,' said Gran Potts, but she saw the look on Peter's face and she said, 'But I'm not cross now, am I?'

'No,' said Peter.

Then he showed Gran his picture. 'That's you looking smiley, Gran. That's Grandad asleep in Dad's deckchair. That's me on the Friday Policeman's bicycle, and that's the Friday Policeman up in the tree, picking apples.'

'What's he doing?' said Dad.

'Picking apples,' said Peter.

Dad dashed out into the garden.

'What's the matter?' asked Peter.

'My apples!' cried Dad. 'Peter's picked nearly all my apples. They weren't ripe yet. They shouldn't have been picked for weeks.'

'It wasn't me,' said Peter, quickly. 'It was the Friday Policeman.'

'I . . . I . . . I . . .' Dad stuttered, going red in the face.

'Now, Dad,' said Gran Potts. 'You know you mustn't be cross with the Friday Policeman, don't you? You're just like me, you look much nicer when you're not being cross.'

'Gran's right, Dad,' said Peter. 'Would you like me to paint a picture of you not being cross?'

'Not just now, thank you very much, Peter,' said Dad, and Gran Potts told Peter to tell the Friday Policeman that picking apples specially for her was a nice idea, but next time to wait until they were ripe, and ask Dad first.

'He says he will,' said Peter.

'He'd better!' said Dad.

'Don't be cross,' said Gran Potts. 'I'm sure he's a nice Friday Policeman at heart.'

'Very nice,' said Peter.

That night, when Gran Potts was giving him his play bath, Peter said, 'I'm very sorry about the mop bucket, Gran.'

'Don't worry,' said Gran Potts.

'And the cushion. And the paint water. And the apples.'

'I'm sorry if you think I'm cross all the time, Peter,' said Gran Potts.

'Don't worry about it, Gran,' said Peter.

'I'll tell you what I'm going to do, Peter,' said Gran Potts. 'I'm going to take you and baby Paula out to the park tomorrow. We'll go to the play area, and we'll get ice-creams

72

and I'll play with you and I won't be cross!'

'*Lovely*, Gran,' said Peter, and he went to bed thinking about it, and how nice it was going to be.

6   The Saturday Pirates

Wham! Crash! Wallop! BANG!

'Good morning, Grandad,' said Mum, sitting down on the end of Grandad's bed.

'Morning,' muttered Grandad, sleepily.

Wham! Crash! Wallop! Bang! KER-PLUM!

'What's all the noise?' said Grandad, sleepily.

'That is Peter and his pirates,' said Mum.

'Pirates?' said Grandad.

'The Saturday Pirates,' said Mum. 'Peter closed his eyes, spun round three times, said:

"WHO IS THERE
UNDER THE STAIR?"

and two pirates popped out. One is called

Morgan and the other is called Blackbeard. Peter informs me that Morgan is a Good Pirate and Blackbeard is a bad one. They are fighting in the hall and Peter is joining in. Gran Potts says please will you come downstairs and do something about it! She says it was your magic that started all this, and she doesn't want to take two pirates with her to the park.'

'I'll come down,' said Grandad.

Wham! Crash! Wallop! Bang! Kerplum! AAAAAAGH!

The fight was still going on when Grandad came downstairs and Peter and Morgan the Good Pirate were winning.

'You're making a lot of noise, Peter,' said Grandad.

'It isn't me making the noise,' Peter said, and he told Grandad all about Morgan the Good Pirate and Blackbeard the Bad Pirate. 'There are bits of chopped up Pirate all over the hall!'

'Tell them to stop it,' said Grandad. 'Gran doesn't like the noise.'

'Stop it, Pirates,' said Peter. He listened very carefully, and then he said. 'Blackbeard says he'll cut your head off, Grandad.'

'That isn't very nice of Blackbeard,' said Grandad.

'Blackbeard is bad,' said Peter. 'He cuts off arms and noses.'

'And legs,' said Morgan the Good Pirate, who was sharpening his sword on the bannisters. 'Blackbeard cuts off legs, too, Peter.'

'Blackbeard cuts off legs, Grandad,' Peter said. 'He would cut off Paula's leg, if he caught her.'

Mum was coming down the stairs, holding baby Paula, and she heard what Peter said.

'Don't say that, even as a joke, Peter!' Mum said. 'Nobody is going to cut off Paula's leg! I wouldn't let them.'

'Or mine,' said Peter. 'You wouldn't let Blackbeard cut off my leg, would you?'

'No leg cutting off in this house, Peter,' said Mum, firmly.

'Your Mum is right, Peter,' said Grandad, when Mum had gone away. 'You'd better tell your Pirates to behave themselves, or Gran won't take them to the park.'

'I will,' said Peter, and he told Morgan.

'That's all right,' said Morgan. 'But what about Blackbeard?'

At half past eleven, Gran Potts put Paula in Peter's old pram and they set off for the park. Peter came too, in Morgan's Pirate ship, keeping a look-out for Blackbeard.

Blackbeard was sailing along in his ship, on the other side of the hedge, and halfway to the park he started throwing sharp knives.

'Blackbeard is throwing knives at us, Gran,' Peter said.

'I hope he misses,' said Gran.

'Oh!' said Peter. 'He's cut off your ear, Gran!'

'Ouch!' said Gran.

'I've rescued your ear, Gran,' said Peter. 'It was pinned to the ground by one of Blackbeard's knives. Will I sew it back on?'

'Yes,' said Gran Potts. 'Sew it back on for me.'

Peter sewed it back on. 'There!' he said. 'That looks great!'

'I can still hear through it,' said Gran Potts.

'I knew you would be able to. Morgan told me,' said Peter. 'He has to sew lots of pieces back on his Pirates after Blackbeard battles.'

'Thank Morgan very much for his expert help,' said Gran Potts.

Blackbeard's head popped up over the hedge. He had a red nose and great big squashy ears like cauliflowers and a black

beard. He saw Gran Potts, the pram with
Paula in it, Peter, and Morgan the Good
Pirate. He threw another of his sharp knives.

Whizzonk!

'Blackbeard has chopped off Paula's ear!'
Peter announced.

'No he hasn't !' said Gran Potts, in a tired
voice. 'I've had enough of this silly game of
yours, Peter. I'm not taking pirates to the
park! If you want to play with them we'll go
home!'

Peter wasn't pleased.

'What about Morgan?' he said. 'Can Morgan come? Morgan doesn't throw sharp knives.'

Gran Potts remembered that she was supposed to be taking Peter to the park for a treat, and she had promised not to be cross. 'All right. Morgan can come. But he's got to be a very good pirate and behave himself!'

Morgan was very pleased.

When Peter got to the park he went to the sandpit to dig for Blackbeard's treasure. He dug a very big hole, but he didn't find it. He dug another one, and then he went to speak to Gran Potts, who was showing off baby Paula to Mrs. Mantle, the lady who looked after the play area.

'Gran,' Peter said. 'I can't find Blackbeard's treasure. Could you help me to dig?'

'Ask your friend Morgan to help you dig,' said Gran, who had been so busy all week that she was tired out, and hadn't any strength left for digging.

'Tell her I have to polish the cannonballs,' said Morgan. 'Tell her she *has* to help you.'

'Morgan can't help me,' said Peter. 'He is

very busy. He has to polish cannonballs. He says you *have* to help me, Gran.'

'Tell Morgan I won't,' said Gran. Then she saw the look of disappointment on Peter's face and she said, 'I think it's time we went over to the shop and got some ice-cream, Peter, don't you?'

'Stay and dig,' said Morgan. 'Digging is important.'

'Morgan says I have to stay here and dig, but you can bring me back my ice-cream from the shop,' Peter said. 'I'd like a raspberry, please.'

'You should go with your Gran, Peter,' said Mrs. Mantle.

'Never mind,' said Gran Potts. 'You stay here, Peter. I'll wheel Paula across in the pram all by myself.'

'Nonsense, Mrs. Potts,' said Mrs. Mantle. 'I'll look after the baby for you here. And Peter will help me. Won't you Peter?'

'Morgan won't let me, Mrs. Mantle,' said Peter. 'Morgan is the Pirate Captain and I have to do what he says and he says I have to go and dig.'

Peter and Morgan went off to dig, and Gran Potts went to get Peter's raspberry ice cream, and Paula stayed with Mrs. Mantle.

'I don't want to dig any more, Morgan,' said Peter, after a while.

'Neither do I,' said Morgan.

They traced Morgan's sign in the sand.

Morgan told Peter that he always made his Pirate Sign wherever he went, so that other Pirates would know where he'd been. They traced it with Morgan's sword and then Peter said: 'What are we going to do now, Morgan?'

'There's going to be a battle,' Morgan said. 'We're going to sail round the world and follow Blackbeard the Bad Pirate to his Treasure Island. We'll have a battle and I'll cut off Blackbeard's head.'

'I want to cut off Blackbeard's head,' said Peter.

'All right,' said Morgan. 'You can borrow my sword.'

Peter started making practice swishes with the sword.

Sssssssssh!

Swiiiiiiish!

Zrrrrrrrrm!

'Peter!' shouted Mrs. Mantle. 'What do you think you are doing with that spade?'

'It isn't a spade,' said Peter. 'It's Morgan's sword and he lent it to me so that I could practise cutting heads off.'

'Nonsense!' said Mrs. Mantle. 'You're standing there throwing sand round you! Look what you've done to Anna Frances.'

Anna Frances was standing beside Mrs. Mantle, rubbing her eyes and crying.

'There now,' said Mrs. Mantle. 'Don't rub the sand into your eyes, dear, or you'll make it worse.' Then Mrs. Mantle turned back to Peter. 'You're a bad boy!' she said. 'How would you like someone to throw sand in your eyes? I'll have to take Anna Frances to the shelter. You can look after your little sister when I'm gone. Don't you dare leave her for a minute!'

Mrs. Mantle went off to the shelter with Anna Frances.

'I don't want to look after Paula,' Peter said to Morgan.

They were supposed to be sailing round the world on Morgan's Pirate ship, following Blackbeard to his Treasure Island, having a battle, cutting Blackbeard's head and ears and legs and nose and knees off, and taking all his treasure. They couldn't do that *and* look after Paula in her pram.

Morgan had an idea. He told Peter about it and Peter wasn't sure, but Morgan said it would be all right, so they did it.

Mrs. Mantle had told Peter not to leave Paula, but Morgan said they weren't going to leave her, they were going to take Paula with them.

They set sail from the sandpit, wheeling Paula in her pram and heading into a stiff breeze, their sails set for the Spanish Main, the battle with Blackbeard, and Treasure Island.

Meanwhile, out on the High Seas, Black-beard sailed on, not knowing that he was being followed. He sailed right across the play area, and Morgan and Peter sailed after him, stopping only long enough for Morgan to scratch his Pirate Signs.

It was in the bushes that pushing the pram became difficult. Peter couldn't squeeze it between the branches.

'No babies in battles!' Morgan said, and then he told Peter to leave Paula on his Pirate Island, where she would be safe, and Black-beard couldn't get at her to cut off her ears.

'Babies don't like battles, Paula,' Peter told her, and he left her.

They sailed on straight into a big storm and half way through the big storm Blackbeard attacked and there was a terrible battle. Mor-gan's ship charged right across the play area with Morgan and Peter waving their swords and firing cannonballs and banging with their pistols and getting ready to cut throats and make people walk the plank. Then Peter fell into the sea and was attacked by crocodiles and he bit one's head off and then he jumped on another one and hit it on the nose CRUMPPP! and Blackbeard saw him and

came leaping down into the sea to attack him
and they were fighting and punching and . . .

'Peter!' shouted Gran Potts. 'Peter! Come
here this minute, Peter!'

Peter came across to the shelter where Gran
Potts was standing with a worried-looking
Mrs. Mantle.

'Did you bring my raspberry ice-cream,
Gran?' Peter asked.

85

'Peter, where is Paula?' Gran Potts said.

'Morgan says babies aren't allowed in battles so I didn't bring her. I left her . . .'

'LEFT HER!' interrupted Mrs. Mantle. 'I TOLD you not to leave her. I swear I did, Mrs. Potts. I told that naughty boy not to leave her. He left little Paula, and now the poor baby is lost!'

Mrs. Mantle started running round the play area, looking for Paula and the pram and Gran Potts said: 'You must NEVER leave the baby again, Peter. Anything could have happened to her.'

'Morgan said she would be all right,' said Peter, biting his lip, which was beginning to feel trembly. 'Morgan said Paula would be safer if we left her, because babies aren't allowed in battles.'

'Don't say another word about Morgan!' Gran Potts said. 'Do you understand? Morgan is made up. Your little baby sister Paula is real, Peter, and you've lost her!'

'I didn't lose her,' said Peter, sounding as if he was going to start crying. 'Morgan said she would be all right if we left her on his Pirate Island.'

'Where?' said Gran Potts.

86

'On Morgan's Pirate Island,' said Peter.

'Peter, is Morgan's Pirate Island a *real* place? Can you find it?' Gran Potts asked, anxiously.

'I don't know the way,' Peter said.

'We'll have a look for it, shall we?' said Gran Potts, and she took Peter by the hand, and they went back to the sand pit where Peter's sea voyage had started.

'Look, Gran!' said Peter, and he pointed at Morgan's Pirate Sign.

'There's another one,' he said, going to the flower bed. 'This must be the way we went!'

They went on through the bushes. Peter didn't remember which way to go, but he was able to follow Morgan's Pirate Signs, and they went on and on through the bushes following the signs until . . .

'Paula!' cried Gran Potts.

There was baby Paula, fast asleep in her pram, amid the bushes where Peter had left her.

'This is Morgan's Pirate Island,' said Peter.

Gran Potts picked Paula out of the pram and hugged her, and then she hugged Peter.

'You're my baby too, Peter,' she said.

Peter cuddled up against her, very relieved that Gran Potts wasn't cross with him.

'I'm not a baby,' he said. 'I'm a boy.'

'That right!' said Gran Potts. 'You're my grandson, and Morgan is your pirate, and together you've kept baby Paula safe. I'm not going to be cross with you, but you must never do such a thing again, understand?'

'I understand,' Peter said.

'I expect it was mostly Morgan's fault,' said Gran Potts.

'You don't believe in Morgan,' Peter said.

'Don't I?' said Gran Potts. 'Who made the Secret Signs, then? The ones we followed to find Morgan's Pirate Island?'

'Morgan did!' said Peter.

Gran Potts bought Peter another raspberry ice-cream to replace the one that had gone drippy when they were searching for Paula, and then they all sailed home in Morgan's Pirate Ship, taking Blackbeard the Bad Pirate with them as a prisoner.

Gran Potts didn't tell Mum and Dad and Grandad about losing Paula, and so none of them ever knew.

Peter meant to tell Felixstowe about it that night, but Felixstowe didn't come to sit in her usual place on the end of his bed. Instead, she looked into the room as he was going to sleep, and whisked her tail at him.

'Goodnight, Felixstowe,' said Peter, sleepily, and Felixstowe slipped away, because she had something extra special to do that Peter didn't know anything about.

7   The Sunday Surprise

Sunday was another busy day, because Gran Potts and Grandad were going home.

Peter helped Gran Potts to pack her tooth glass and her apron and her slippers. Then she took him down to the kitchen and made him a special fizzy drink.

Peter helped Grandad to pack his pipe and his tobacco. Then Grandad took him to the shops and bought him a comic.

Dad made everybody a mid morning snack, and then Peter and Dad drove Gran Potts and Grandad down to the station. Peter got a platform ticket and waved to Gran Potts and Grandad as the train was going out and then Dad took him to the snack bar and bought him another fizzy drink and a cheese sandwich, but the cheese sandwich was curled up a bit and Peter didn't eat it.

'Dad,' said Peter, as they were going home. 'Do you think there'll be anyone in my House under the stairs today?'

'What do you think?' said Dad.

'I don't think so,' said Peter.

'Why not?' said Dad.

'I think the magic was to do with Grandad,' said Peter.

'I think you're right,' said Dad.

'There probably won't be anyone under the stairs, now Grandad's gone,' said Peter, when he got home to Mum.

'Do you think so?' said Mum. 'I don't!'

'Don't you?' said Peter.

'No,' said Mum. 'I think there *might* be a surprise for you under the stairs today, Peter, if you look very hard.'

'Do I have to close my eyes and spin round three times and say:

'WHO IS THERE
UNDER THE STAIR?'

asked Peter.

'Of course,' said Mum. 'Otherwise the

House under the stairs' magic won't work, will it?'

So Peter closed his eyes, spun round three times, and said:

'WHO IS THERE
UNDER THE STAIR?'

and opened the door under the stairs.

At first, he couldn't see anything.

'There's nothing there, Mum,' he said, in a disappointed voice.

'Are you sure, Peter?' said Mum. She came over to the little door under the stairs and opened it wider and Peter saw, right in the farthest corner of the little house, all curled up in the blankets,

One ...

two ...

three ...

four ...

five ...

little furry bundles, with shiny black noses, and tightly shut eyes, and little wriggly tails.

'What are they, Mum?' asked Peter.

'Kittens!' said Mum. 'They're your Sunday Surprise, arranged by very special magic with Felixstowe.'

'Can I play with them?' asked Peter.

'Not today,' said Mum.

'Oh,' said Peter. He was used to Dragons and Witches and Wozzles and Robbers and Policemen and Pirates coming out of the House under the stairs, and he'd been able to play with them.

'They'll be big enough to play with in a few days time,' said Mum.

'Won't they go away?' said Peter.

'Not for ages and ages, until they're grown up,' said Mum. 'Then we'll have to find good homes for them. They'll be here tomorrow, and the day after that, and for lots of days after that, in the House under the stairs.'

'They're *real* kittens, aren't they, Mum?' said Peter, still not certain that it wasn't House under the stairs' magic.

'Real kittens.' Mum agreed.

'I like real kittens,' said Peter. 'They're much better than magic ones.'

Felixstowe slipped past them, in to the House under the stairs, and lay down beside her kittens.

'Are they Felixstowe's babies, Mum?' asked Peter.

'Yes,' said Mum.

94

'I was your baby, wasn't I, Mum? Just like Paula?'

'You're both my babies,' said Mum.

'Felixstowe's babies aren't magic though, are they Mum?'

'All babies are magic,' said Mum.

'What sort of magic?' asked Peter.

'Making-happy magic,' said Mum. 'Just listen to Felixstowe!'

Felixstowe was purring and purring with happiness, as she lay beside her kittens in the House under the stairs.

'I don't mind Felixstowe having my house until her kittens grow up,' said Peter.

'Good,' said Mum.

'It's a very magic House under the stairs, Mum,' said Peter, 'isn't it?'

And Mum agreed that it was.